To my children,

May my life serve as an example to you that any goal you set
or any dream you may have is possible to achieve.
Keep God first and know that every obstacle I overcome is so you may never have to.

Love,
Daddy

To Caley, Mommie's "little princess": I love you!

Terrell's Acknowledgments

I would like to thank my family for their undying love and support, my literary agent Ian Kleinert for believing in me, Todd Harris for his exceptional work, Glenn Yeffeth for his patience, and everyone at BenBella Books for all of their hard work and dedication to making this project a success.

To Courtney Parker, not only a writing partner but a true and lifelong friend. Thank you for your support over the years. I am so proud that you have stayed committed to your craft and am honored to have had the opportunity to be a part of seeing your dreams come to fruition.

Courtney's Acknowledgments

Thank you to Ian Kleinert, Glenn Yeffeth, and Todd Harris; you all are truly amazing!

To my family and friends: thank you for always sharing your stories. I love you!

To Kristel Crews and my new family at Wolf Films: you're the best! To Margarita Mayorga: thanks for taking such great care of Caley. To Bishop Kenneth C. Ulmer and Pastor Tony Gardner: thank you for keeping me fed with God's word (Pastor Gardner, your words "literally" saved my life). To the entire BenBella staff: what a joy this has been for me; you've been a blessing.

Terrell, you'll never know how much you and our friendship over the years have meant to me. Even in the midst of trials, true friendship always prevails. Beyond measure, you are loved.

Todd's Acknowledgments

A big thanks to my parents; if it weren't for them I would not be able to see the merit in doing this book.

To my friends and family and all my respected colleagues, who make me a better artist and a better person.

To Terrell and Courtney, who showed enough trust in me to bring the vision from their minds to paper and for being so gracious and open in the creative process.

Lastly, to all the great people at BenBella Books, for making this an amazingly smooth and enjoyable experience.

Note to the Reader

This project has truly been a blessing for us from start to finish.
We hope every parent and child reading this book will be equally as blessed.

 BenBella Books, Inc., 6440 N. Central Expressway, Suite 617, Dallas, TX 75206
www.benbellabooks.com • Send feedback to feedback@benbellabooks.com

Printed in the United States of America
10 9 8 7 6 5 4 3 2

Library of Congress Cataloging-in-Publication Data is available.
ISBN 193377120-8

Cover design by Laura Watkins • Interior design and composition by John Reinhardt Book Design • Printed by Bang Printing

Distributed by Independent Publishers Group. To order call (800) 888-4741 • www.ipgbook.com

For special sales contact Yara Abuata at yara@benbellabooks.com

Little T Learns to Share

BY
Terrell Owens

WITH
Courtney Parker

Illustrations by
Todd Harris

BENBELLA
BENBELLA BOOKS, INC.
Dallas, TX

Little T was outside
playing with his new football
when along came Sam and Tim,
who hadn't one at all.

They gathered around Little T, to see his something new,
and eagerly they asked him, "Little T, can we play with you?"

Little T looked at his friends, then down at his new ball.
To tell the truth, he hadn't meant to play with them at all.

The ball was fresh out of the box,
the laces were still white—
what if his friends lost it 'cause they didn't catch it right?

He didn't want his ball messed up, so told them with a frown,
"I don't think so, Sam—I'm sorry, Tim—
I'mma have to turn ya'll down.

I just got this ball, and I don't know if you care
but I've got to let you know that I'm not ready to share.
Maybe if you come back later, in a day or two.
Maybe if you come back then, I will play with you."

Sam and Tim, they cried aloud,
"Little T, that's just not fair!
You shouldn't wait
'til something's old
before you learn to share."

But Little T, he clutched his ball, and walked off in a huff.
He shouted back to Sam and Tim,
"I said no; now that's enough!

I don't have to share with you, this is *my* new ball.
I don't have to be that fair, or play with you at all."

Little T walked to his house, new football still in hand.
"I can play in my backyard, alone just like I planned.
I don't need Tim or even Sam, I'll play here by myself.
I don't need to share my ball with anybody else."

Pretty soon he realized he wasn't having any fun.
He really couldn't play without the help of anyone.
When he threw the football, there was no one there to catch.
He couldn't score a touchdown
without someone to score against.

Football is the type of game you need your friends to play,
but Little T feared he might not have his friends after today.

His head hung low, he went inside,
tears forming in his eyes.
"What's wrong, Little T?" his mother asked.
"What happened to make you cry?"

"I got into an argument with Sam and Tim again—
just 'cause I didn't share my ball, now they won't be my friends.

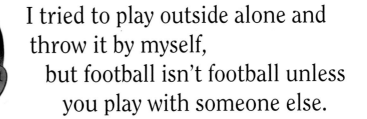

I tried to play outside alone and
throw it by myself,
    but football isn't football unless
    you play with someone else.

Now I think I've ruined it,
I've made a big mistake.
I should've let them play—
    it's just a ball, for
    heaven's sake!"

Little T's mother pulled him close, hearing what this was about.
She agreed with him that he'd been wrong,
and needed to take a "time out."

"You've learned a valuable lesson about always being fair.
It's important to not be selfish, and to always try to share.

When you're blessed with the
chance to do something nice,
or have a chance to give,
take advantage of it, Little T;
being nice is the way to live.

"Now that you've played
all by yourself
and had no fun at all,

I think you should find
Sam and Tim and ask them
to play football.

Apologize to both of them for failing to be fair
and let them know that they were right:
as friends you should always share."

"But what if they won't play with me?"
sniffed Little T as he wiped his eyes.
"You'll never know the answer," she said,
"unless you give it a try."

So Little T, he grabbed his ball, and ran back out to play.
He hoped his friends would forgive him
for what he'd said that day.

He spotted them in Sam's front yard, playing in the grass.
Maybe, he thought, *they'll still want to play that game of pass.*

"Hey guys," he said, "can I talk to you?
There's something I'd like to say.
I wanted to tell you how sorry I am, for how I acted today.

"You were right about my ball, I wasn't being fair.
But now I've learned my lesson and would really like to share."

"No problem," shouted Sam and Tim together. They agreed,
"Of course we'll forgive and play with you—
you're our best friend, Little T!"

The three of them, they played all day.
They kicked and passed the ball.
Once Little T had learned to share, football was fun for all.